Crossing the Sea

Mark Schoenbeck
Genworth Financial Wealth Management

© Genworth Financial Wealth Management
ISBN – 978-1-935165-05-7
Published by SourceMedia
Printed in Mexico

*"To all those dedicated to helping investors
pursue their financial dreams."*

In the lavender light of a new dawn, two married couples emerged from their respective houses and descended a rutted path to a small harbor where two boats sat anchored a few yards from shore. Many of their neighbors were already there waiting, and still more continued to gather. Some smiled in support while others shed soft tears. The two couples exchanged hugs and encouraging words with one another. Anxious and yet hopeful, they were ready to cross the sea.

The couples had worked hard all their lives and each dreamed of retiring to a plot of fertile land where they could plant grapes and olives, and enjoy a peaceful life. But the island on which they lived had grown crowded, the streets overrun with merchants and tradesmen offering their goods, the tillable land sparse. Recently, word had come that good land could be found on an island across the sea, that one need only to make the long journey to claim it.

The first couple had been merchants in their working days, and they believed in the power of prevailing conditions. When pearls had come into fashion, they had commissioned a craftsman to make pearl bracelets and pendants, and added these to their wares. When their neighbors developed a taste for pomegranate wine, they bought all the pomegranate seedlings they could find.

Sometimes, when trends suddenly reversed themselves, they had been left with items they could no longer sell at a profit, but they had held onto them, believing their value would one day rise again.

When word of the available land had reached them, they had looked out over the horizon and noticed a steady wind and calm waters. Holding to what they had

learned as merchants, they believed a boat capable of riding the prevailing wind would be most effective in getting them to the island safely and comfortably.

So they had outfitted a boat with a tall mast and a large sail. That the horizon was also edged with dark clouds did not bother them. They accepted that it might storm occasionally, but believed the fair winds would inevitably return.

The second couple had also been merchants in their working lives. They too had invested in pearls, but at the first indication of a decline in value they sold their entire supply at a reduced price, only to see the value of pearls climb for several more seasons. The craze for pomegranate wine they had avoided altogether, thinking it only temporary. Having watched many trends rise and fall, they knew that current fashions did not always last. In their experience, the key to building wealth was to focus on more reliable endeavors and avoid risk.

They had looked out over the same horizon as the first couple, but had paid little attention to the steady breeze and calm waters. For them, the clouds at the edge of the horizon indicated approaching storms.

They had decided they would not put their faith in the rising and falling winds, that they would instead cross the sea by more consistent means. So they had outfitted a rowboat. They knew this meant making slower progress on the days when the wind blew favorably, but they preferred to make at least some progress every day, no matter the weather.

With the good wishes of their families and neighbors, the couples embarked. As the steady wind was still blowing off the island, the couple in the sailboat took the lead. They exalted in their strategy. The couple in the rowboat pulled on their oars with all their strength, but, as they watched the sailing couple slip ahead, they worried about their slow pace.

After a time, however, conditions changed. The skies grew dark, the winds began to swirl, and the seas turned rough. The sailing couple was tossed about and blown off course. They had to pull down their sail or risk the destruction of their boat. Yes, they had made good progress when the wind had been favorable, but now that they were making no progress, or even moving backward, they doubted their strategy of putting their faith solely in the wind. Soon, the other boat overtook them. It was the rowing couple's turn to celebrate.

For long stretches of time, the weather alternated between fair and stormy. The two couples overtook each other many times. When each was making good progress, they believed their strategy the wisest, and when conditions were not in their favor they grew frustrated. At heart, both couples wished they had more confidence in their strategy and could make more consistent progress.

As the journey continued, many dark nights passed and the two boats lost track of each other. Indeed, neither

couple could be sure they were still on the proper course. The sea was more vast, the journey more eventful, than either imagined.

At long last, the couple in the sailboat reached the promised island. As they scanned for a safe place to come ashore, they noticed the rowboat resting on a sandy beach, the rowing couple lying beside it.

The rowers had arrived the previous day. They'd only had strength enough to pull their boat ashore before collapsing into sleep. But now, at the sound of the sailboat sliding onto the beach, they awoke.

The two couples eyed each other. Everyone was exhausted and tattered from the long and difficult journey, but, overcome by the joy they felt at having arrived, they embraced and supported one another. Both couples climbed the grassy slope above the beach to survey the new land, ready to build their new lives.

They crested a plateau and before them lay a flat, fertile green field. But they were surprised to see it was encircled by a line of large stones.

Within the circle of stones, a boat had been overturned and propped up to create a temporary shelter. Beneath this sat a man and woman tending a fire. The pair looked happy and healthy. The rowing couple and the sailing couple both recognized the pair from their home island. They recalled that, on the day of their departure, they had been among those on the beach, waving goodbye.

Breathless, the two couples begged to know how the pair had arrived on the island ahead of them and in such good shape. The pair explained that they had indeed been on the beach for the couples' departure, and had noticed that one of them had outfitted a sailboat and the other a rowboat. The pair could not decide which of the two types of boats might be best for their own journey, so they had sought the counsel of an experienced ocean navigator.

"I have sailed in many different vessels," he told them. "Some are better for short journeys, some for long, but when you are making the most important journey of your life, you should leave nothing to chance. Outfit

a boat that you can both sail and row. This way, your progress will be consistent, you will be more confident when conditions change, and you will be better prepared for anything the journey might hold." So the pair had taken the man's advice and outfitted a boat with both a sail and oars.

Their journey had also been long and arduous, but during bad weather they had managed to stay on course by rowing. During fair weather they had let their sail carry them along, the drag of their oars slowing them only slightly.

And now, having reached the island safely and realized their life's dream, they were thankful for the sage advice they had received—sail *and* row.

Afterword

As you may have noticed in the preceding parable, the sailing couple had generated wealth in their working life through a "buy and hold" strategy. As a result, they adopted a similar strategy for their journey across the sea. The rowing couple's experience in the market had made them wary of changing conditions, so their strategy for crossing the sea was one of risk aversion. But, as conditions changed, each of the couples suffered periods of doubt about the wisdom of their respective strategy.

During the great bull market from 1982-2000, the "buy and hold" strategy of the sailors worked very well. People who began investing during these years created wealth by riding the prevailing winds. Having little experience with other market conditions, they saw no reason to consider other strategies. As a result, anyone trying to interest investors in a rowing strategy during that period was treated skeptically. But since the bursting of the internet bubble in 2000 and the collapse of the global financial markets in late 2008, rowboats have come back into fashion. People who began investing in the early 2000s have experienced greater volatility and little sustained growth in the market. As a result, they have become more risk averse.

But what does the future hold? Given the ever-changing conditions of the market, it seems clear that, like the third couple in the story, the successful investor of the future will seek professional advice and adopt a strategy that includes both sailing and rowing. Investors working with financial advisors who offer a sound investment process, have access to a variety of portfolio strategists, and utilize multiple approaches to asset allocation should be better equipped to "cross the sea" to whatever destination they desire.